RUDOLPH'S
~ ADVENTURE ~

Manufactured in USA.

8   7   6   5   4   3   2   1

ISBN 1-56173-711-9

Contributing writer: Carolyn Quattrocki

Cover illustration: Linda Graves

Book illustrations: Susan Spellman

Publications International, Ltd.

It's Christmas Eve in Reindeer Land! All the little reindeer are excited because Santa Claus will visit this very night. A blanket of new snow has fallen on the ground. The young reindeer are skating and sledding and building snowmen. What fun it is to play in the winter snow!

Fun for all except one little reindeer. "Look at funny Rudolph!" the others cried. "His nose is bigger and redder than a tomato. And look how it shines!" "I brought my sled to play, too," said Rudolph.

"Well, you can't play with us!" laughed the reindeer. Poor Rudolph! Pulling his sled, he walked sadly away. One shiny tear slipped down his face.

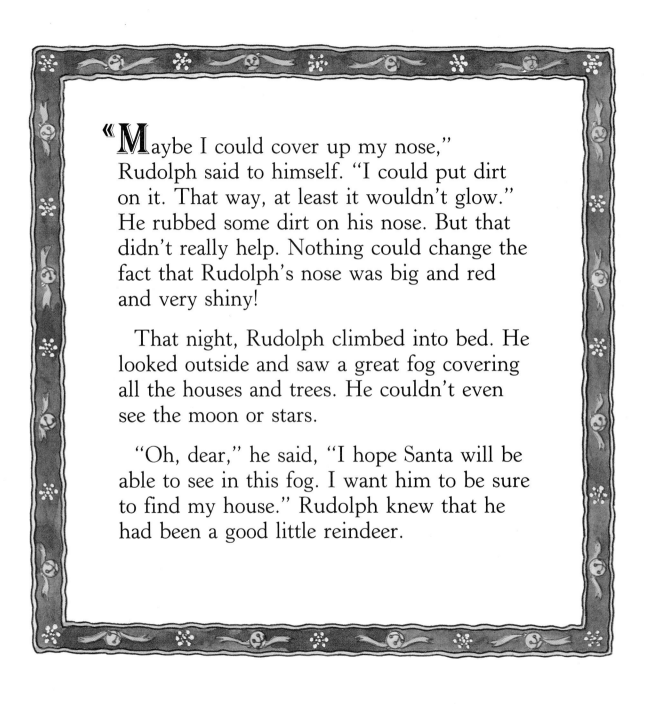

"Maybe I could cover up my nose," Rudolph said to himself. "I could put dirt on it. That way, at least it wouldn't glow." He rubbed some dirt on his nose. But that didn't really help. Nothing could change the fact that Rudolph's nose was big and red and very shiny!

That night, Rudolph climbed into bed. He looked outside and saw a great fog covering all the houses and trees. He couldn't even see the moon or stars.

"Oh, dear," he said, "I hope Santa will be able to see in this fog. I want him to be sure to find my house." Rudolph knew that he had been a good little reindeer.

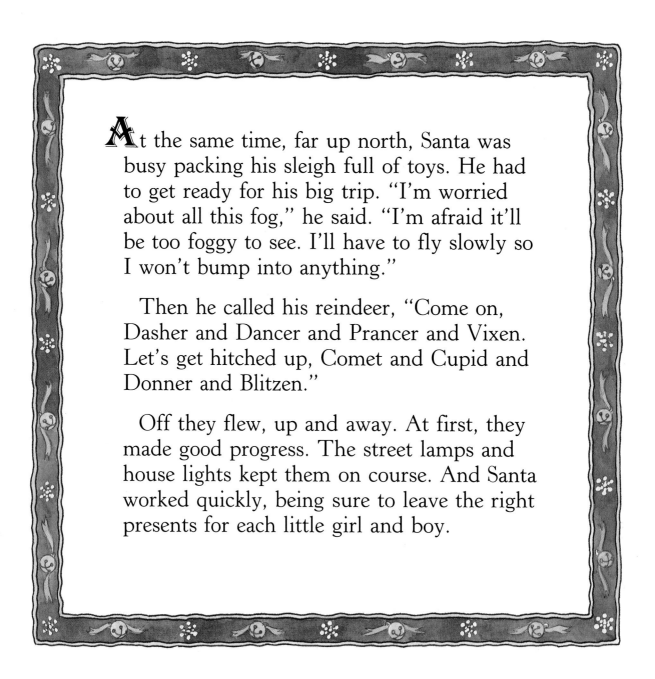

At the same time, far up north, Santa was busy packing his sleigh full of toys. He had to get ready for his big trip. "I'm worried about all this fog," he said. "I'm afraid it'll be too foggy to see. I'll have to fly slowly so I won't bump into anything."

Then he called his reindeer, "Come on, Dasher and Dancer and Prancer and Vixen. Let's get hitched up, Comet and Cupid and Donner and Blitzen."

Off they flew, up and away. At first, they made good progress. The street lamps and house lights kept them on course. And Santa worked quickly, being sure to leave the right presents for each little girl and boy.

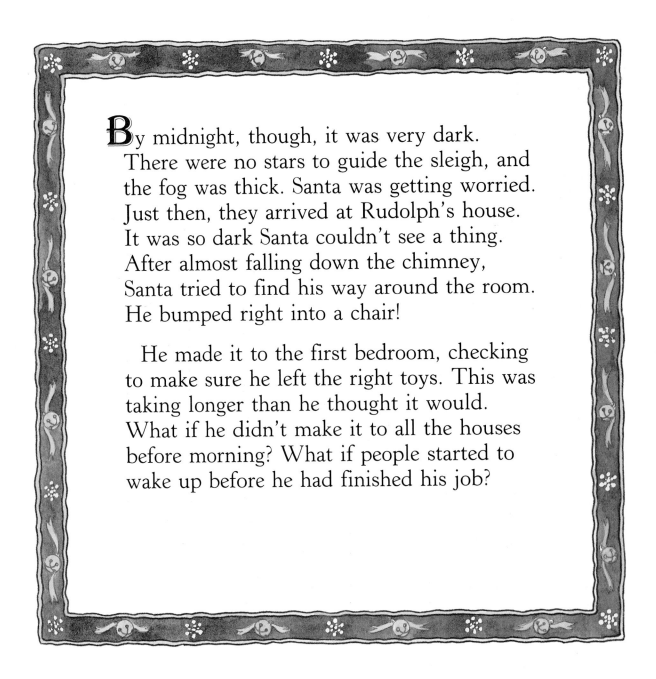

By midnight, though, it was very dark.
There were no stars to guide the sleigh, and
the fog was thick. Santa was getting worried.
Just then, they arrived at Rudolph's house.
It was so dark Santa couldn't see a thing.
After almost falling down the chimney,
Santa tried to find his way around the room.
He bumped right into a chair!

He made it to the first bedroom, checking
to make sure he left the right toys. This was
taking longer than he thought it would.
What if he didn't make it to all the houses
before morning? What if people started to
wake up before he had finished his job?

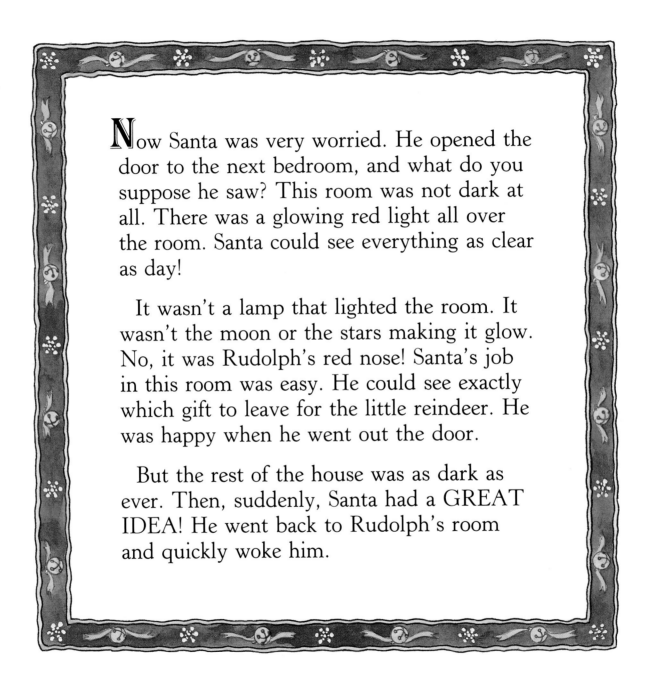

Now Santa was very worried. He opened the door to the next bedroom, and what do you suppose he saw? This room was not dark at all. There was a glowing red light all over the room. Santa could see everything as clear as day!

It wasn't a lamp that lighted the room. It wasn't the moon or the stars making it glow. No, it was Rudolph's red nose! Santa's job in this room was easy. He could see exactly which gift to leave for the little reindeer. He was happy when he went out the door.

But the rest of the house was as dark as ever. Then, suddenly, Santa had a GREAT IDEA! He went back to Rudolph's room and quickly woke him.

Rudolph couldn't believe his eyes. There, right next to his very own bed, was Santa. "Rudolph, you can help me!" said Santa. "The fog and darkness are slowing me down. I might not make it to every boy and girl's house before morning."

"But, what can I do?" asked Rudolph. Santa answered, "I need you to guide us through the fog. Your shiny nose will light the way!" That was all Rudolph needed. Of course he would help. (Wouldn't you?)

Quick as a wink, Rudolph wrote a note to his family. It said, "I've gone to help Santa. Don't worry. I'll be back by morning. Love, Rudolph." Santa dashed away to bring his sleigh down to the lawn so Rudolph could join his reindeer team.

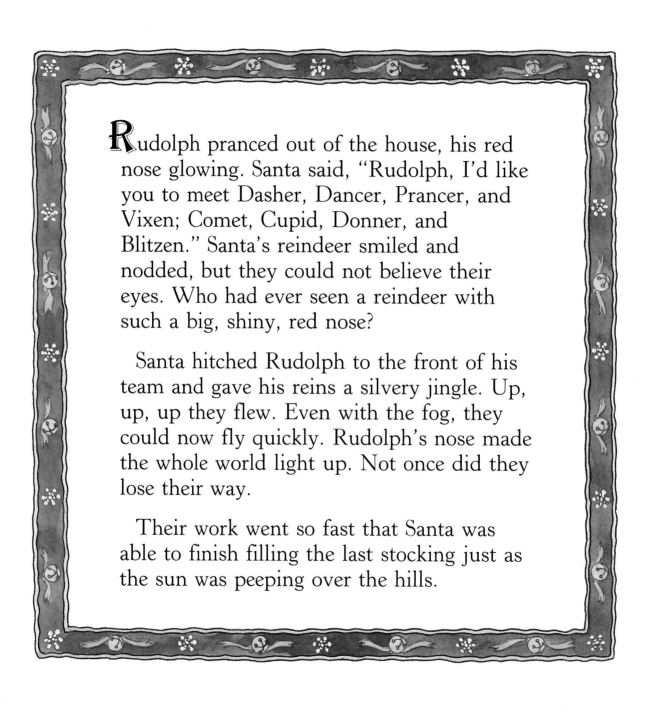

Rudolph pranced out of the house, his red nose glowing. Santa said, "Rudolph, I'd like you to meet Dasher, Dancer, Prancer, and Vixen; Comet, Cupid, Donner, and Blitzen." Santa's reindeer smiled and nodded, but they could not believe their eyes. Who had ever seen a reindeer with such a big, shiny, red nose?

Santa hitched Rudolph to the front of his team and gave his reins a silvery jingle. Up, up, up they flew. Even with the fog, they could now fly quickly. Rudolph's nose made the whole world light up. Not once did they lose their way.

Their work went so fast that Santa was able to finish filling the last stocking just as the sun was peeping over the hills.

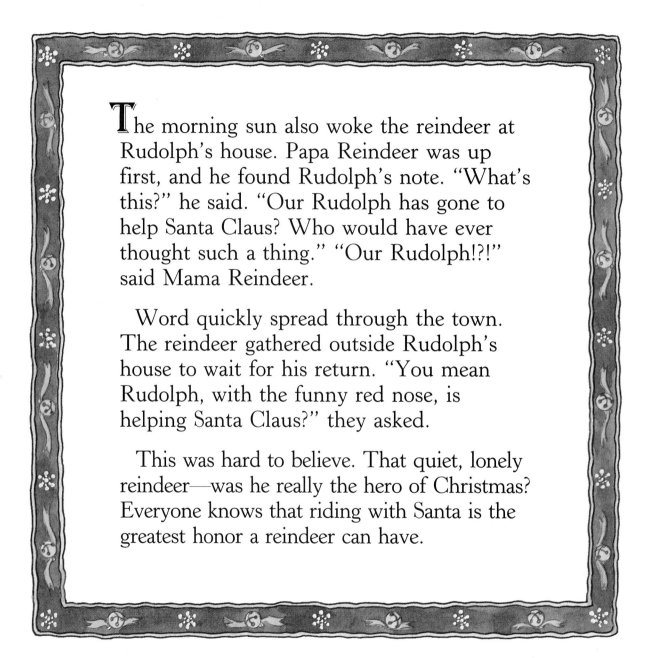

The morning sun also woke the reindeer at Rudolph's house. Papa Reindeer was up first, and he found Rudolph's note. "What's this?" he said. "Our Rudolph has gone to help Santa Claus? Who would have ever thought such a thing." "Our Rudolph!?!" said Mama Reindeer.

Word quickly spread through the town. The reindeer gathered outside Rudolph's house to wait for his return. "You mean Rudolph, with the funny red nose, is helping Santa Claus?" they asked.

This was hard to believe. That quiet, lonely reindeer—was he really the hero of Christmas? Everyone knows that riding with Santa is the greatest honor a reindeer can have.

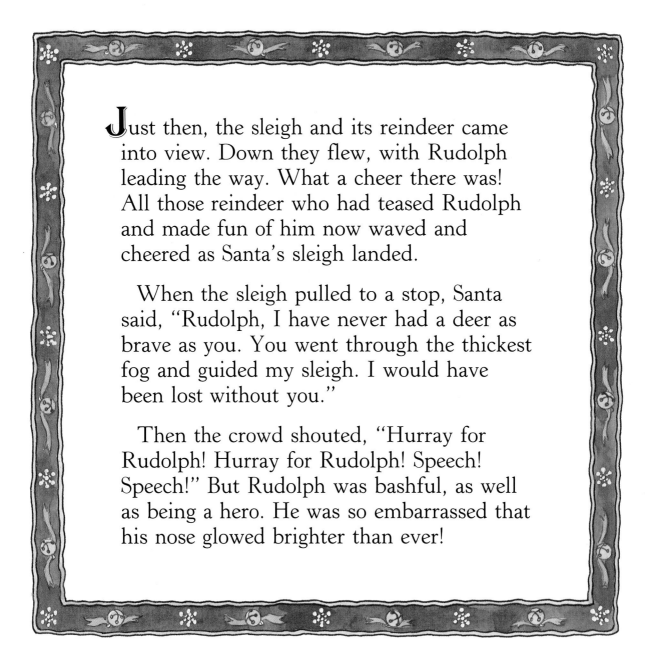

Just then, the sleigh and its reindeer came into view. Down they flew, with Rudolph leading the way. What a cheer there was! All those reindeer who had teased Rudolph and made fun of him now waved and cheered as Santa's sleigh landed.

When the sleigh pulled to a stop, Santa said, "Rudolph, I have never had a deer as brave as you. You went through the thickest fog and guided my sleigh. I would have been lost without you."

Then the crowd shouted, "Hurray for Rudolph! Hurray for Rudolph! Speech! Speech!" But Rudolph was bashful, as well as being a hero. He was so embarrassed that his nose glowed brighter than ever!

If you are very quiet
one foggy Christmas night,
you may hear sleigh bells
and see a bright red light.
You'll know for sure it's Santa,
if on the roof you hear,
the quiet pitter patter
of his tiny reindeer.

For Naomi, Joe, Eddie,
Laura and Geraldine

M.R.

Text copyright © 1986 by Michael Rosen
Illustrations copyright © 1986 by Quentin Blake
All rights reserved including the right of
reproduction in whole or in part in any form.
First published in Great Britain in 1986 by Walker Books Ltd.
Published by Prentice-Hall Books for Young Readers
A Division of Simon & Schuster, Inc.
Rockefeller Center
1230 Avenue of the Americas
New York, NY 10020

10 9 8 7 6 5 4 3 2 1

10 9 8 7 6 5 4 3 2 1 pbk

Prentice-Hall Books for Young Readers
is a trademark of Simon & Schuster, Inc.
Printed in Italy

Library of Congress Cataloging in Publication Data
Rosen, Michael, 1946—
Under the bed.
Summary: Poetry and prose about bedtime and sleep,
from both children's and parents' viewpoints.
[1. Bedtime—fiction.   2. Bedtime—Poetry]
I. Blake, Quentin, ill.   II. Title.
PZ7.R71867Un   1986   86-11268
ISBN 0-13-935412-3

MICHAEL ROSEN AND QUENTIN BLAKE

UNDER THE BED

PRENTICE-HALL BOOKS FOR YOUNG READERS
A Division of Simon & Schuster, Inc.
New York

Fooling Around

"Do you know what?"
said Jumping John.
"I had a bellyache
and now it's gone."

"Do you know what?"
said Kicking Kirsty.
"All this jumping
has made me thirsty."

"Do you know what?"
said Mad Mickey.
"I sat in some glue
and I feel all sticky."

"Do you know what?"
said Fat Fred.
"You can't see me,
I'm under the bed."

After Dark

Outside after dark
trains hum and traffic lights wink
after dark, after dark.

In here after dark
curtains shake and cupboards creak
after dark, after dark.

Kêu Kan Ket
cót Ket

Under the covers after dark
I twiddle my toes and hug my pillow
after dark, after dark.

Things You Say

What If...

What if
my bed grew wings and I could fly away in my bed.
I would fly to the top of a big tall building,
look out over all the streets
and then come floating slowly down to the ground.

I would fly to a misty island near Japan
and watch fishing boats cross the sea.

If my bed grew wings I would fly to a thick forest
where there was an old broken-down castle
that no one knew about, hidden in the trees.
And wherever I went
and whatever I saw,
all the time I was in my bed.

Things They Say

Nat and Anna

Anna was in her room.
Nat was outside the door.
Anna didn't want Nat to come in.

Nat said, "Anna? Anna? Can I come in?"
Anna said, "I'm not in."

Nat went away.
Anna was still in her room.
Nat came back.

Nat said, "How did you say you're not in?
You must be in if you said you're not in."
Anna said, "I'm not in."
Nat said, "I'm coming in to see if you're in."
Anna said, "You won't find me because I'm not in."
Nat said, "I'm coming in."

Nat went in.

Nat said, "There you are. You are in."

Anna said, "Nat, where are you?
Where are you, Nat?"
Nat said, "I'm here."

Anna said, "I can't see you, Nat. Where are you?"
Nat said, "I'm here. Look."
Anna said, "Sorry, Nat. I can't see you."
Nat said, "Here I am. I'm going to scream, Anna.
Then you'll see me."
Anna said, "Where are you, Nat?"
Nat said, *"Yaaaaaaaaaaaaaaaaaaaa!"*
Anna said, "I can hear you, Nat. But I can't see you."
Nat said, "Right. I'm going out. Then you'll see me."

Nat went out.

Nat said, "Anna? Anna, can you see me now?"
Anna said, "No, of course I can't, you're outside."
Nat said, "Can I come in and see you then?"
Anna said, "But I'm not in."

Nat went away screaming.
He didn't come back.

These Two Children

There were these two children
and they were in bed and it was
time they were asleep.

But they were making a huge noise,
shouting, yelling and screaming.
"Look at me!" "Look at you!"
"Let's go mad!" "Yes, let's go mad!"

Their dad heard them and
he shouted up to them,
"Stop the noise! Stop the noise!
If you don't stop the noise, I'm
coming upstairs and I'll give
you a bit of real trouble."

Everything got quiet.

A few minutes later one of the
children called out,
"Dad, Dad, when you come up to give
us a bit of real trouble, can you bring
us up a drink of water as well?"

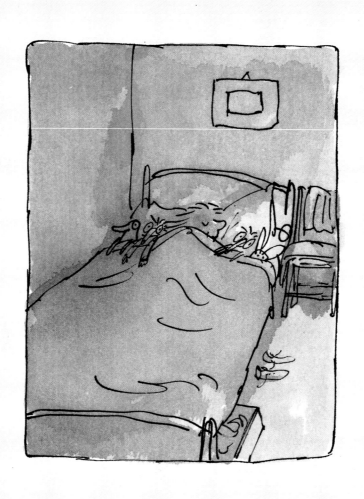